We're Sailing Down the Nile
A Journey through Egypt

In memory of my mother, Lydia — L. K.

For Charlie and all his adventures yet to come — A. W.

The author has been fortunate in receiving both information and encouragement from Dr. Lanny Bell,
Professor of Egyptology, Brown University; and Mr. Magdi Shalash, Egyptologist, Cairo, Egypt. Many thanks.

Barefoot Books
2067 Massachusetts Ave
Cambridge, MA 02140

First published in the United States
of America in 2007 by Barefoot Books Inc

Graphic design by Louise Millar, London

Color separation by Grafiscan, Verona
Printed and bound in China by PrintPlus Ltd

This book was typeset in Amigo and Legacy

The illustrations were prepared in printed collaged
papers with acrylic and painted backgrounds

1 3 5 7 9 8 6 4 2

Library of Congress Cataloging-in-Publication Data

Krebs, Laurie.
    We're sailing down the Nile : a journey through Egypt / Laurie
Krebs ;
[illustrated by] Anne Wilson.
    p. cm.
    Summary: As the riverboat sails down the Nile River, remnants of
Egypt's long history and aspects of its present culture are revealed on
its banks.
    ISBN-13: 978-1-84686-040-9 (hardcover : alk. paper)
    [1. Nile River--Fiction. 2. Egypt--Description and travel--Fiction.
3. Stories in rhyme.]   I. Wilson, Anne, 1974-   , ill. II. Title. III.
Title:
We are sailing down the Nile.
PZ8.3.K867We 2007
[E]--dc22
                                                              2006023464

We're Sailing Down the Nile

A Journey through Egypt

written by Laurie Krebs

illustrated by Anne Wilson

Barefoot Books
Celebrating Art and Story

Climb aboard the river boat! We're sailing down the Nile.

Ra

Hawk

We'll visit Abu Simbel in just a little while.

We see the temple just ahead. Jabari's in the lead.

Amun

Ram

We stand before the statues, feeling very small indeed.

Climb aboard the river boat! We're sailing down the Nile.

Bastet

Cat

We'll shop at Aswan's market in just a little while.

Kalila guides us to the souk*. We buy some food to share.
*marketplace

Isis

Cow

We'll picnic on the Island* with the others gathered there.

*Kitchener's Island

Climb aboard the river boat! We're sailing down the Nile.

Thoth

Ibis

We'll reach the Valley of the Kings in just a little while.

Our pharaohs once were buried here, says Ibrahim with pride,

Serket

Scorpion

And Tutankhamen's tomb was found with treasures packed inside!

Climb aboard the river boat! We're sailing down the Nile.

Anubis

Jackal

We'll be at the Oasis* in just a little while.

*Al-Faiyum Oasis

Zahara greets the farmers, who are harvesting their crops.

Geb

Goose

They'll take their fruit and vegetables to sell in village shops.

Climb aboard the river boat! We're sailing down the Nile.

Sobek

Crocodile

We'll see the Cairo skyline in just a little while.

Inside the vast museum halls, we see fantastic things.

Khepri

Scarab
Beetle

Mustafa spies the mummies of the crocodiles and kings.

Climb aboard the river boat! We're sailing down the Nile.

Seshat

Leopard

We'll hike to Giza's pyramids in just a little while.

Jamilah knows these wondrous tombs, built centuries ago,

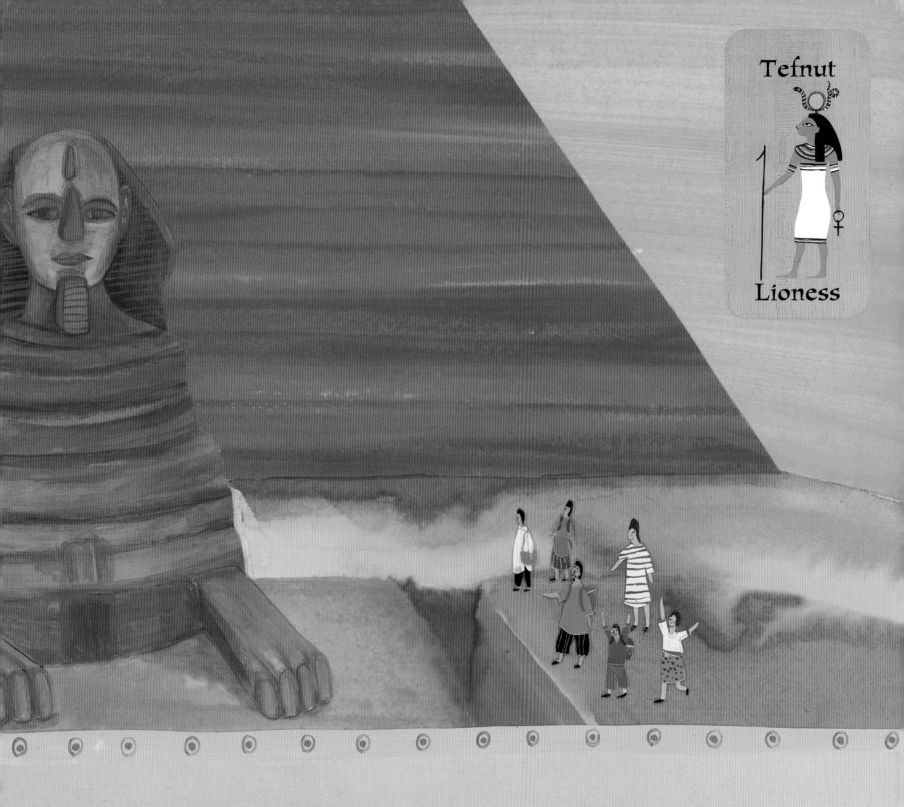

Still rise above the city, with the fabled Sphinx below.

Climb down from the river boat! We've sailed along the Nile,
And traveled across Egypt for just a little while.

Nut

Water

The day is nearly over and the sun sets in the west.
We'll dream about our journey and the places we loved best.

Mediterranean Sea
ISRAEL
JORDAN
EGYPT
Cairo
Giza
LOWER EGYPT
UPPER EGYPT
SAUDI ARABIA
LIBYA
Eastern Desert
Nile River
Al-Faiyum Oasis
Valley of the Kings
Luxor
Red Sea
Aswan
Kitchener's Island
Aswan Dam
Western Desert
Abu Simbel
Lake Nasser
SUDAN

Our Journey

You can follow our journey down the Nile with this map of Egypt. Here are some facts about the places we visited:

 Abu Simbel's ancient monuments were moved to safety from Lake Nasser's rising water during the 1960s. It was a UNESCO triumph of technology.

 Aswan, a beautiful town on the Nile, is Egypt's southern-most city. Its exotic marketplace, Sharia as-Souq, has welcomed caravans and shoppers for centuries.

 Kitchener's Island is one of two major islands near Aswan. It is a popular spot for weekend picnics or a quiet afternoon away from the busy city.

 The **Valley of the Kings'** tombs were built below ground to discourage thieves. Tutankhamen's tomb was discovered in the 1920s.

 Al-Faiyum Oasis is home to more than two million people. It is called the Garden of Egypt because of the fruits and vegetables grown there.

 Cairo, Egypt's capital, is a crowded, bustling city. The world-famous Egyptian museum has exhibits dating from before the Old Kingdom to the Roman Empire.

 The Great Pyramid of Giza, Cheops, is one of the Seven Wonders of the World. The mysterious Sphinx has a human head and a lion's body.

The History of Ancient Egypt

For more than three thousand years, Egypt ruled the civilized world. Scholars have divided its history into time periods that help us understand its story.

Early Dynastic Period
(c. 3000–2575 BC)

At first, there were two parts to the country: Upper Egypt and Lower Egypt. Each had its own king, or pharaoh. Quite early on in this period, Upper and Lower Egypt joined to form one kingdom.

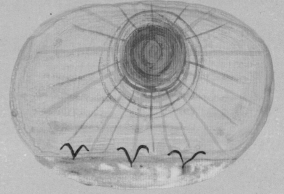

First Intermediate Period
(c. 2150–2040 BC)

Egypt fell on hard times. Nile floods did not always bring enough water for food crops. Hunger and unhappiness spread among the people. As the pharaoh's power collapsed, the country split into many small states.

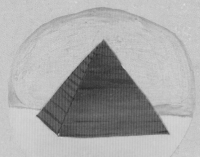

Old Kingdom
(c. 2575–2150 BC)

Pharaoh was considered a god who controlled the rising sun each day and the flooding Nile each year. Many of Egypt's great stone pyramids, or tombs, were built during the Old Kingdom.

Middle Kingdom
(c. 2040–1640 BC)

After a long time, Egypt became one country again. The pharaohs developed trade routes and repaired canals and harbors. It was a time of peace.

Second Intermediate Period
(c. 1640–1540 BC)

A series of weak rulers allowed foreigners, the Hyksos, to invade Egypt. They introduced Egypt to chariots, horses, new tools and weapons.

Third Intermediate Period
(c. 1070–664 BC)

Times changed, and two powers emerged. Pharaohs ruled from the northern cities, while priest-kings ruled from the southern temples of Thebes. The empire began to shrink.

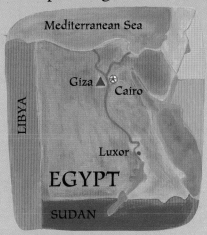

New Kingdom
(c. 1540–1070 BC)

The Hyksos were forced from Egypt. Pharaohs conquered new lands, which brought fresh ideas and great wealth to the country. This was Egypt's Golden Age. Many famous pharaohs — Queen Hatshepsut, Akhenaten, Tutankhamen and Ramesses II — lived during this time.

Late Period
(c. 664–332 BC)

In the Late Period, power shifted between Egyptian pharaohs and foreign kings. In 332 BC, Alexander the Great, a Greek, conquered Egypt. The Age of Pharaohs ended, and Egypt was ruled by other countries until it became independent in modern times.

Life in Ancient Egypt

Picture a pyramid. Egyptians were divided into social groups that mirrored this shape.

At
the top
was Pharaoh,
the king.
His word was law.

Beneath him were priests, nobles
and government officials, who
carried out Pharaoh's wishes.

Next came the professional class: scribes, doctors
and artisans, who were well trained for their jobs.

Below them were peasants: the farmers and laborers
who did most of the hard work.

At the bottom of the pyramid were slaves who worked in the households of the rich.

What Did Ancient Egyptians Do?

Here are a few examples of the jobs of the Ancient Egyptians:

Architects designed Pharaoh's temples, tombs, pyramids and palaces.

Priests and Priestesses honored the gods with ceremonies in the temple. They brought gifts to the gods and sang songs of praise to please them.

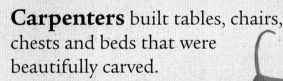

Carpenters built tables, chairs, chests and beds that were beautifully carved.

Scribes kept records, counted taxes and wrote letters for Pharaoh.

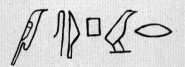

Doctors treated broken bones, wounds and diseases with splints, bandages and ointments. They used magic spells too.

Sculptors created statues for temples and tombs, using ordinary tools and working with wood and stone. Some statues were painted.

Glassmakers molded and cut glass to form perfume jars, beads and vases, all with colorful designs.

Jewelers worked mostly for the wealthy, using gold, studded with gemstones, to create elaborate designs.

Soldiers fought with bows and arrows, spears and axes. At first they carried just a leather shield but later, metal strips were added to their tunics for protection.

Potters made jugs, pots and bowls for everyday use. Objects were made in shades of blue or turquoise to match the gemstones that Egyptians loved.

Weavers wove a plant called flax into linen cloth. People used it for clothing because it was light and comfortable in the hot Egyptian weather.

Mummies and Pyramids

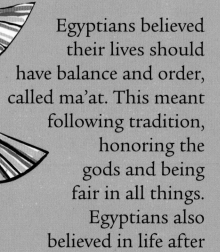

Egyptians believed their lives should have balance and order, called ma'at. This meant following tradition, honoring the gods and being fair in all things. Egyptians also believed in life after death, but they needed their earthly bodies so that their spirit would have a place to live. Preserving the body was the job of a mummy-maker, called an embalmer. He removed the person's organs and placed them in special jars. Using a kind of salt, he dried the body and then packed it with rolls of linen, sawdust and spices. After several weeks, the body, or mummy, was wrapped in strips of linen, with magic charms tucked between the layers.

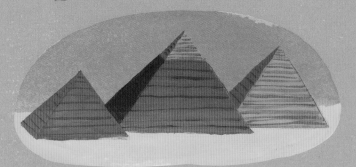

Three pharaohs were buried in the Great Pyramids at Giza between 2600 and 2500 BC. Everything they needed in the next world was buried with them, including furniture, clothing, food, jewelry and pottery. The first pyramid was built for King Cheops. It is said that it took 100,000 men twenty years to build the tomb. A second pyramid, nearly the same size, was built for his son, King Chephren. Visitors today can see his black granite coffin in the burial chamber. The smallest of the three pyramids was built for King Mycerinus, who was probably the grandson of Cheops and the son of Chephren.

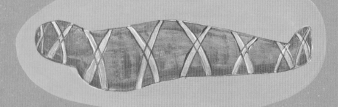

During his last days, the dead person would have memorized spells for protection. Now the mummy was ready for the dangerous journey to the underworld. Copies of the spells were packed in the dead person's tomb or painted on its walls in case he was forgetful.

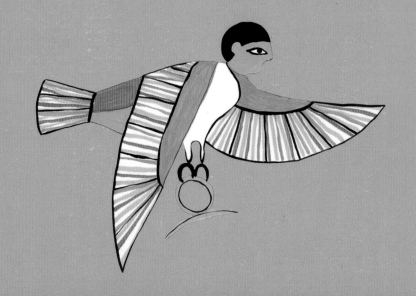

The Mighty Floods

The Flooding of the Nile

Egyptian villages and farms were nestled along the Nile River, and the people planned their lives by its changing rhythm. Each July, water from heavy rains and melting snows in the Ethiopian highlands reached the Nile and caused the river to overflow its banks. In many ways, this was good news because the floods brought fresh, rich soil to the farmlands. By October, the river had drawn back, and farmers planted their crops, watering them from storage basins. By late May, the ground was dry and parched again.

The people waited anxiously, hoping their god, Hapy, would send the yearly floods. To make sure he did, they held festivals in his honor. When the rains began, everyone watched the water level carefully. Too much would sweep away homes and ruin farms; too little would yield poor harvests and not enough food. The right balance, or ma'at, was needed for life to run smoothly.

Two Lands

Ancient Egyptians called the fertile Nile Valley the Black Land. Their crops were nourished by the rich, dark soil of the yearly floods. Around the Black Land was Egypt's hot, dry desert, called the Red Land. This area provided the salt for mummy-makers, as well as many kinds of stone and precious metals. Today, the colors of the Black and Red Lands are still in use. They are two of the colors of the Egyptian flag.

The Aswan Dam

In 1965, the Aswan High Dam was built and Egyptian life changed forever. No more unpredictable floods. No more drought and hunger. The river brought a steady supply of water.

Building the dam has brought many benefits. It produces electricity for the country. It encourages farmers to grow crops all year, not just after the floods. It allows desert to be turned into farmland.

But some not-so-good things have happened too. Part of Egypt's coastline has been washed away, along with much of its marine life. Farmers have to use artificial fertilizer because rich soil is no longer left by the floods. Ancient buildings are threatened by high water levels. The government continues to work on solving these problems.

Gods and Goddesses

Gods and goddesses were central to life in Ancient Egypt. Each day, temple priests held ceremonies to please them. Gods and goddesses were often shown as humans with animal features. There are many Egyptian gods and goddesses. Here are the ones you will find in this story.

Amun, "god of the sky." Amun was pictured as a man wearing a ram's horns or a crown topped by two tall feathers. In later years, he joined the sun god Ra and became Amun-Ra, the King of Gods.

Geb, "god of the earth." Geb was called "The Great Cackler" and laid the egg from which the Earth was hatched. He was drawn as a goose or as a man with a goose on his head.

Anubis, "god of the underworld." Anubis guided the dead on their journey to the next world. He was seen as a reclining jackal or as a human with a jackal's head.

Isis, "queen of the throne." Isis was the symbolic mother of Pharaoh. On her head, she carried either a sun disc tucked inside cow's horns or a throne.

Bastet, "daughter of Ra." Bastet had the head of a fierce lioness. In time, she became a kindly goddess, with the head of a cat.

Khepri, "the creator." Sporting a scarab beetle on his head, Khepri was the sun god who created each new day. He pushed the sun disk across the sky, much as a beetle pushes a dung ball across the ground.

Nut, "goddess of the sky." Pictured with her body arching over the sky from horizon to horizon, Nut often balanced a water pot on her head.

Seshat, "the record keeper." Seshat was the goddess of writing, measurer of time and scribe to the king. Clothed in leopard skin, she wore a headdress containing a seven-pointed star.

Ra, "father of the gods." The sun god, Ra, rose from the underworld each morning, traveled across the sky and re-entered the underworld at night. He was shown as a man with a hawk's head.

Sobek, "god of the water." Sobek was depicted as a man with the head of a crocodile. People feared and respected this powerful god, just as they feared and respected the crocodile itself.

Tefnut, "goddess of moisture." The goddess Tefnut was portrayed as a lioness with a serpent atop her head.

Serket, "goddess of healing." Serket protected Egyptians from deadly scorpion stings. She wore a long-tailed scorpion on her head and was shown in tomb scenes as guarding the dead.

Thoth, "god of the scribes." Thoth was the god of writing and counting. He often appeared as a man with an ibis head.

Egyptian Scripts

Hieroglyphs

Thousands of years ago, Egyptians created a written language using pictures called hieroglyphs. Sometimes drawn on clay tablets, each picture stood for an object, an idea or a sound. At first, hieroglyphs were used to record business deals. Later, they decorated the walls of temples and tombs with stories about the gods and pharaohs.

Reading hieroglyphs was a puzzle, even for scribes who studied them. There were hundreds of symbols and difficult grammatical rules to learn. Some texts were read from left to right, some from right to left and some from top to bottom. There were no vowels or punctuation. Drawing hieroglyphs was slow and difficult.

Eventually a script, called hieratic, was created for everyday use. Drawing the script with pen and ink on sheets of paper, called papyrus, was much quicker than carving hieroglyphs in stone.

Demotic Script

In time, an even fancier kind of writing, demotic script, was invented. It had no hint of hieroglyphic pictures. Its signs flowed together in a stream, moving from right to left in horizontal rows. For more than a thousand years, the script was used for important documents.

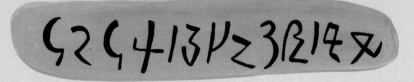

The Rosetta Stone

After years and years, new languages were spoken in Egypt and people could no longer read hieroglyphs. Scholars tried, but the meaning of the pictures remained a mystery. Then, in 1799, a French soldier, digging a fort along the Nile River, uncovered an ancient stone tablet that we now call the Rosetta Stone. Words on the stone were written in hieroglyphs, demotic script and Greek. When scholars translated the Greek, they thought the other scripts must tell the same story. Jean-François Champollion, a French scholar, studied the stone and figured out the connection between the demotic scripts and hieroglyphic symbols. At last, the mystery of Egyptian hieroglyphs was solved!

Barefoot Books
Celebrating Art and Story

At Barefoot Books, we celebrate art and story that opens
the hearts and minds of children from all walks of life, inspiring
them to read deeper, search further, and explore their own creative gifts.
Taking our inspiration from many different cultures, we focus on themes that
encourage independence of spirit, enthusiasm for learning, and sharing of
the world's diversity. Interactive, playful and beautiful, our products
combine the best of the present with the best of the past to
educate our children as the caretakers of tomorrow.

Live Barefoot!
Join us at *www.barefootbooks.com*